JACK's Fantastic Voyage

*For Captain Philip Moran, Master Mariner,
whose house in St. Ives inspired this story*

JACK's Fantastic Voyage

MICHAEL FOREMAN

Red Fox

A Red Fox Book

Published by Random House Children's Books
20 Vauxhall Bridge Road, London SW1V 2SA

A division of Random House UK Ltd
London Melbourne Sydney Auckland
Johannesburg and agencies throughout the world

First published in 1992 by Andersen Press Ltd

Red Fox edition 1994

© Michael Foreman 1992

Printed in Hong Kong

RANDOM HOUSE UK Limited Reg. No. 954009

ISBN 0 09 930138 5

JACK'S mother and father both worked in the city, so Jack spent his holidays with his grandfather, a sea captain, in his old house by the sea. Jack loved it there.

The house was very old and made of wood. It looked like a beached boat. A strong wind could send sea-spray, full of salt and sand, flying over the roof into the narrow street behind.

YET it was the inside of the house that held the most
wonders for Jack. His grandfather had painted pictures
everywhere. When he had grown too old to sail the seas he
painted his memories.

The beams of the ceiling were carved and hung with

wooden birds and the floorboards carved with fishes. All around the sides of Grandfather's big bed were scenes of wild seas and shipwrecks. On the panel above the pillows was an ocean of icebergs. At the foot of the bed was mounted a great ship's wheel.

D URING the day, Jack often played with his friends on the beach, but it was the evenings that Jack loved best. That was when Grandfather told him the stories behind the pictures.

Starting out as a young ship's boy, Jack's grandfather had lived a life of adventure. He seemed to have sailed every sea and visited every port. Jack loved his descriptions of tropical islands, the air thick with scents, spices and parrots. In his imagination he saw great whales spouting, and dolphins and flying fishes around Grandfather's ship.

Most of all, Jack looked forward to stormy nights because then Grandfather told his terrifying tales of typhoon and shipwreck.

Bᴜᴛ one day, while playing with his friends, Jack heard some of them laughing about his grandfather.

"Look out Jack! Here comes your crazy grandad!"

"He's not crazy! I love him," said Jack.

"He's bonkers! Paints mad pictures and makes up stories!"

"He doesn't make them up," cried Jack.

"Of course he does. He's never even been to sea! You ask anyone," shouted one of the boys, and they all ran off as Grandfather approached.

"Had a good time, Jack?" asked Grandfather, smiling. Jack hoped that Grandfather had not heard what the boys had been saying.

THAT evening, when Grandfather told Jack another story of the sea, he made it sound so real that Jack felt sure he could not be making it up.

Next door to Grandfather's house was a tiny bookshop. The owners were Grandfather's closest friends and sometimes looked after him when he was ill. They often took him bowls of hot soup but if the bowls were left there too long Grandfather painted ships all over them.

"Surely," thought Jack, "they will know the truth about my grandfather."

Next morning Jack went to the bookshop.

"Well, Jack," said Mr Andersen, the bookshop owner, "your grandfather hasn't been to sea since we've known him. But he is the oldest person in the village. Maybe he had all his adventures before we met him."

Jack just didn't know what to think.

The next day, Jack didn't go to the beach with the other boys, but spent the day on the rocks close to Grandfather's house. Grandfather knew something was troubling him, and that evening he cooked him his favourite supper of fresh brill and crinkley chips.

WHEN the dishes were washed and stowed away,
Grandfather tucked Jack up in the big bed and
began another tale.

It was a tale to match the night. A tale of storm and
danger amongst icebergs and frozen seas. The wind was
buffeting the shutters, and waves full of stones rattled
on the roof. The house shook. Grandfather moved the
dishes from the shelves to the cupboards underneath, but
still continued with the story.

"The ship's boy was now at the wheel, trying to hold her
into the wind." He turned to Jack.

"Take the wheel, Jack." Half asleep, Jack crawled to the
ship's wheel at the foot of the bed.

"It was a dark and stormy night!" continued Grandfather.
"It took all the boy's strength to keep the wheel steady.
Hold her steady, Jack!" he shouted over the storm.

J ACK could feel the house shaking. Swaying from side to side. Books fell from the shelves and a chair slid across the floor. The storm shutters were now off the windows.

Jack could see the light from the distant lighthouse. It seemed to be bouncing in the dark. The house was afloat!

GRANDFATHER raced downstairs to the kitchen. Jack heard him shovelling coal into the big black cooking range. "We need more steam!" he cried. "Keep her steady, Jack! To the left of the light."

They were beyond the harbour, pitching over the white topped waves.

As they neared the lighthouse, a thick blanket of fog rolled over them and only the mournful sound of the lighthouse foghorn told Jack where to steer. It was a comforting sound and reminded him of Grandfather snoring.

Under the fog the sea was not so rough. Jack began to

feel at ease with the wheel. He got used to the shift and sway. Grandfather was now on the balcony outside the front window, peering into the mist. Sometimes, without turning round, he raised his arm and pointed left or right, and Jack changed course.

THEN the fog thinned and was gone. Instead of black rolling waves there was a white sea of ice and a sky full of stars.

They sailed slowly through a zig-zag channel in the ice
until they entered an ocean of blue and green water dotted
with huge icebergs.

AND there they were. All the ships from Grandfather's paintings. The great clippers with their white sails,

fast cutters and schooners, brown sailed smacks and
luggers, and even the grimy collier from the coal bucket.

FOR hours they sailed among this magic fleet and around every iceberg. Seals were chased by polar bears; whales and narwhals rose and fell in the clear water.

THEN ice began to close over the sea and the ships were gone. They sailed back through the zig-zag channel and

it shut behind them. The blanket of fog covered everything once more.

WHEN Jack woke up, the pale sun was just appearing over the horizon. He dressed and went onto the balcony. Everything seemed normal. The house was high and dry

amongst its neighbours. Had it all been just a dream?
He went to find his grandfather to tell him all about it.

JACK found him at the back of the house. He could
hardly believe his eyes. There was Grandfather,
standing on a chair, chipping the last tell-tale
icicle off the roof.